W9-CPP-793
Worm
Skywriting with Worm
Me as a baby
Found this cool meteorite

For Cory and Jessica

—D.C.

For my beautiful niece, Maddy. I love you.

—H.B.

Joanna Cotler Books is an imprint of HarperCollins Publishers.
Diary of a Fly Text copyright © 2007 by Doreen Cronin
Illustrations copyright © 2007 by Harry Bliss
Manufactured in China.
For information address HarperCollins Children's Books,
a division of HarperCollins Publishers, 10 East 53rd Street,
New York, NY 10022.
www.harpercollinschildrens.com Library of Congress
Cataloging-in-Publication Data Cronin, Doreen. Diary of a
fly / by Doreen Cronin ; pictures by Harry Bliss. — 1st ed.
p. cm. Summary: A young fly realizes, day by day, that there
is a lot to learn about mastering flight school and getting along
with 327 brothers and sisters, and she discovers that heroes
come in all shapes and sizes.
ISBN 978-0-06-000156-8 (trade bdg.) — ISBN 978-0-06-000157-5
(lib. bdg.) — ISBN 978-0-06-223298-4 (paper-over-board)
[1. Flies—Fiction. 2. Diaries—Fiction.]
Bliss, Harry, date, ill. II. Title. PZ7.C88135Dfl
2007 2006036064 [E]—dc22 CIP AC Typography
by Neil Swaab 12 13 14 15 16 SCP 10 9 8 7 6 5 4
First Edition

DIARY OF A FLY

By Doreen Cronin

Pictures by Harry Bliss

Joanna Cotler Books

An Imprint of HarperCollins*Publishers*

JUNE 7

Tomorrow is the first day of school. I'm so nervous. What if I'm the only one who eats regurgitated food?

JUNE 8

Great news! Everyone eats regurgitated food!

JUNE 10

Things they teach you in flight class:

We are the most accomplished fliers on the planet.

Our average speed is 4.5 mph.

Leap backward when taking off.

Things they should teach you in flight class:
Always have a flight plan.

JUNE 12

My parents left us with a babysitter last night. When they got home, eighty-seven of us were stuck to a strip of flypaper.

Mom says we were
a lot easier to watch
before we grew heads.

JUNE 14

Today we practiced landing on moving targets.

I am standing on her head right now.

JUNE 15

My school picture came out terrible.

Mom says next time I better have all my eyes looking in the same direction.

JUNE 17

My first science assignment is to use my five senses to observe something creepy. I chose a first grader.

JUNE 18

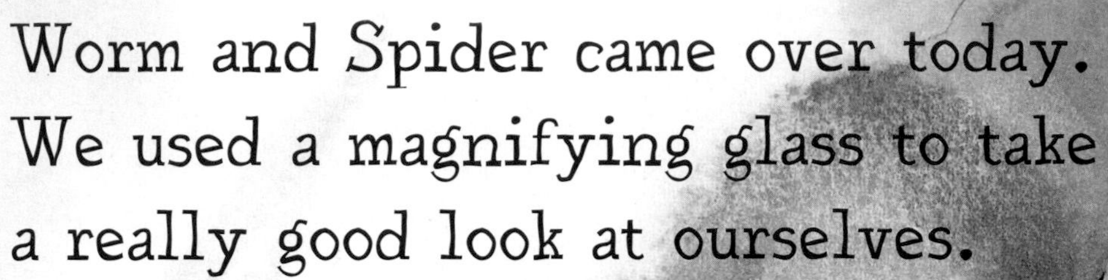

Worm and Spider came over today. We used a magnifying glass to take a really good look at ourselves.

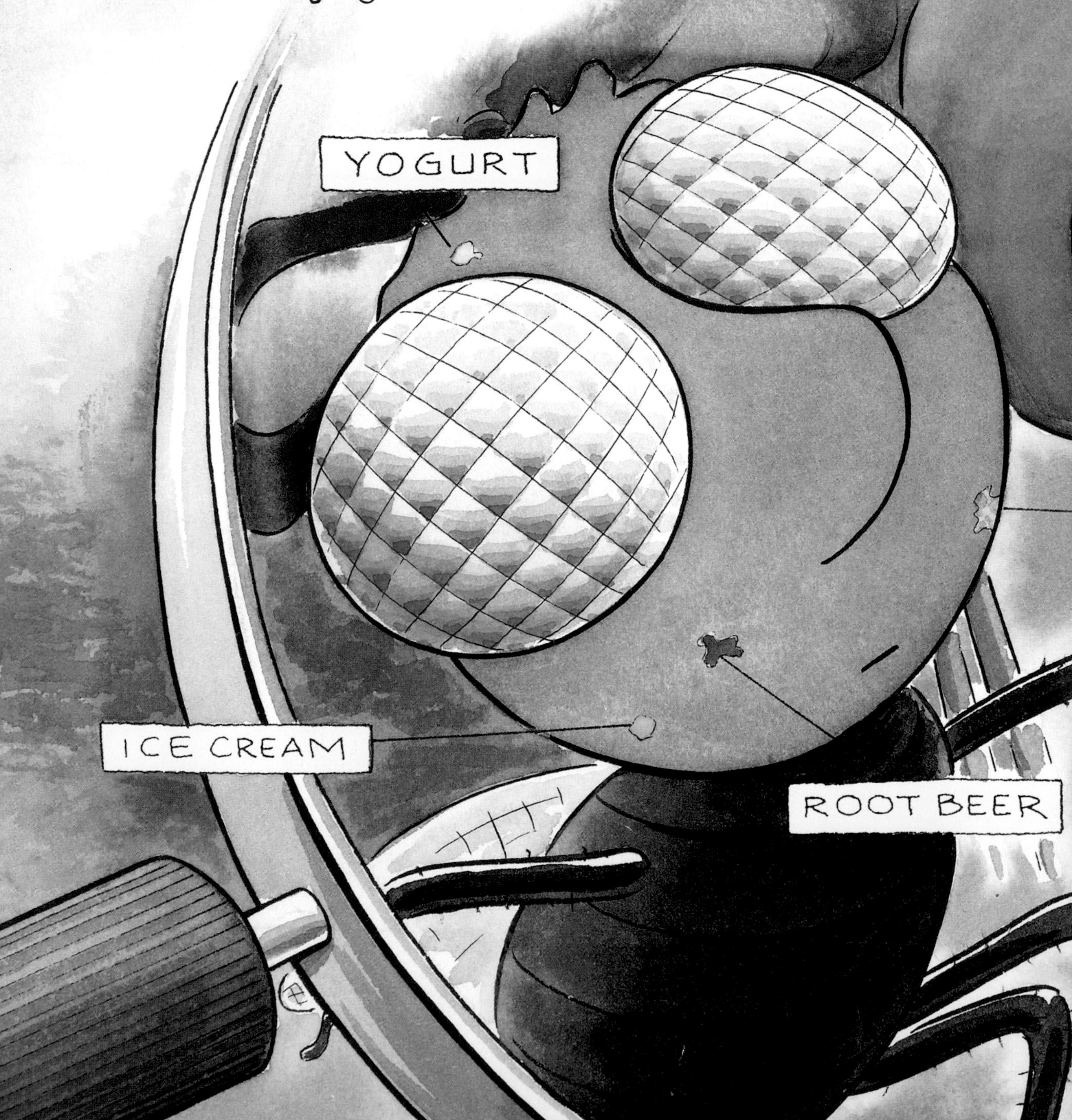

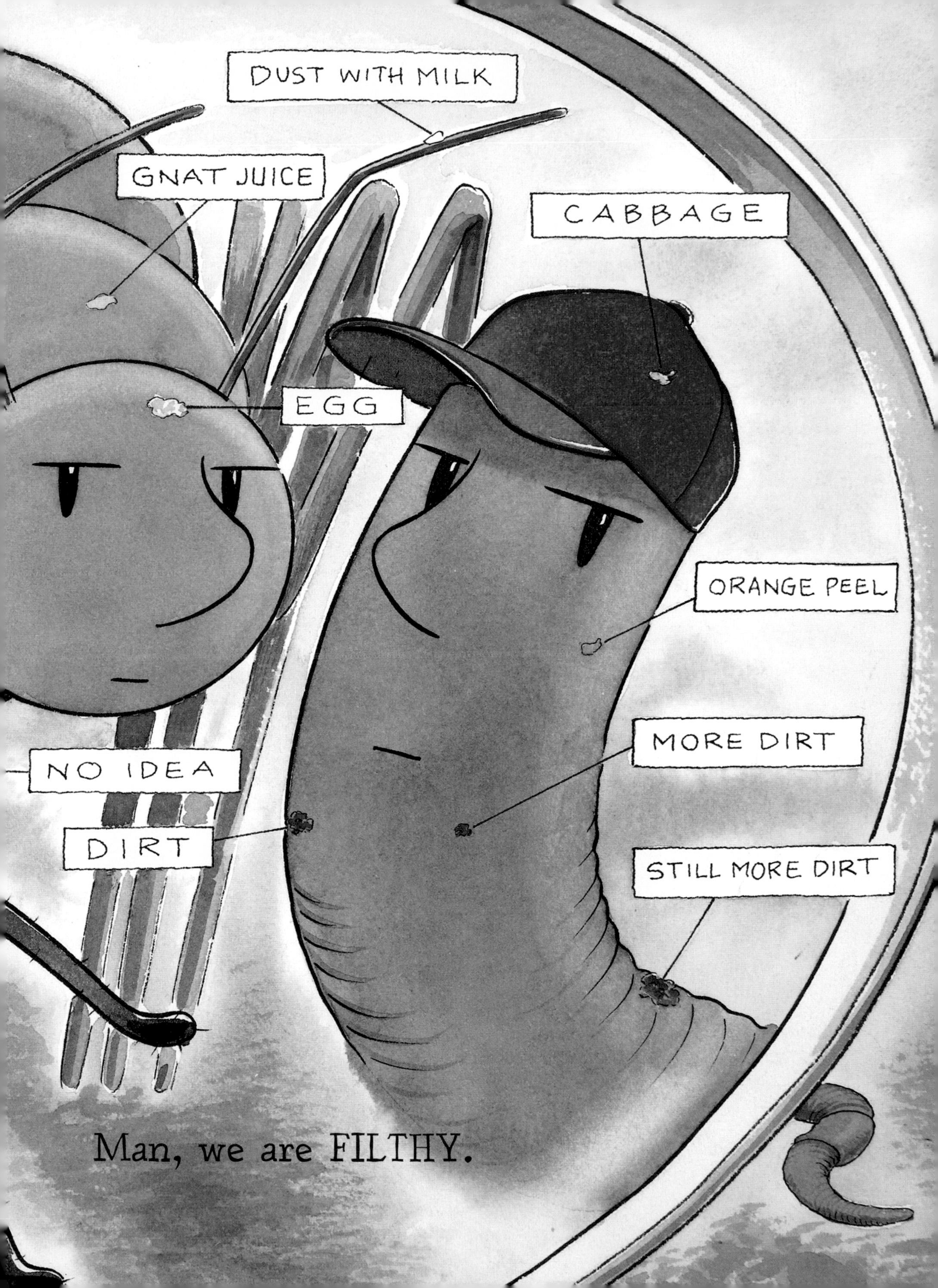

Man, we are FILTHY.

JULY 2

I'm making an "All About Me" book for my mom:

DAY 5:
First day as a maggot
DAY 7:
First day with a head
worm
DAY 10: First day of School!
School
LUNCH

JULY 13

I asked my mom why I can't have my own room like Worm.

I told her we could put half of them in the garage to save space.

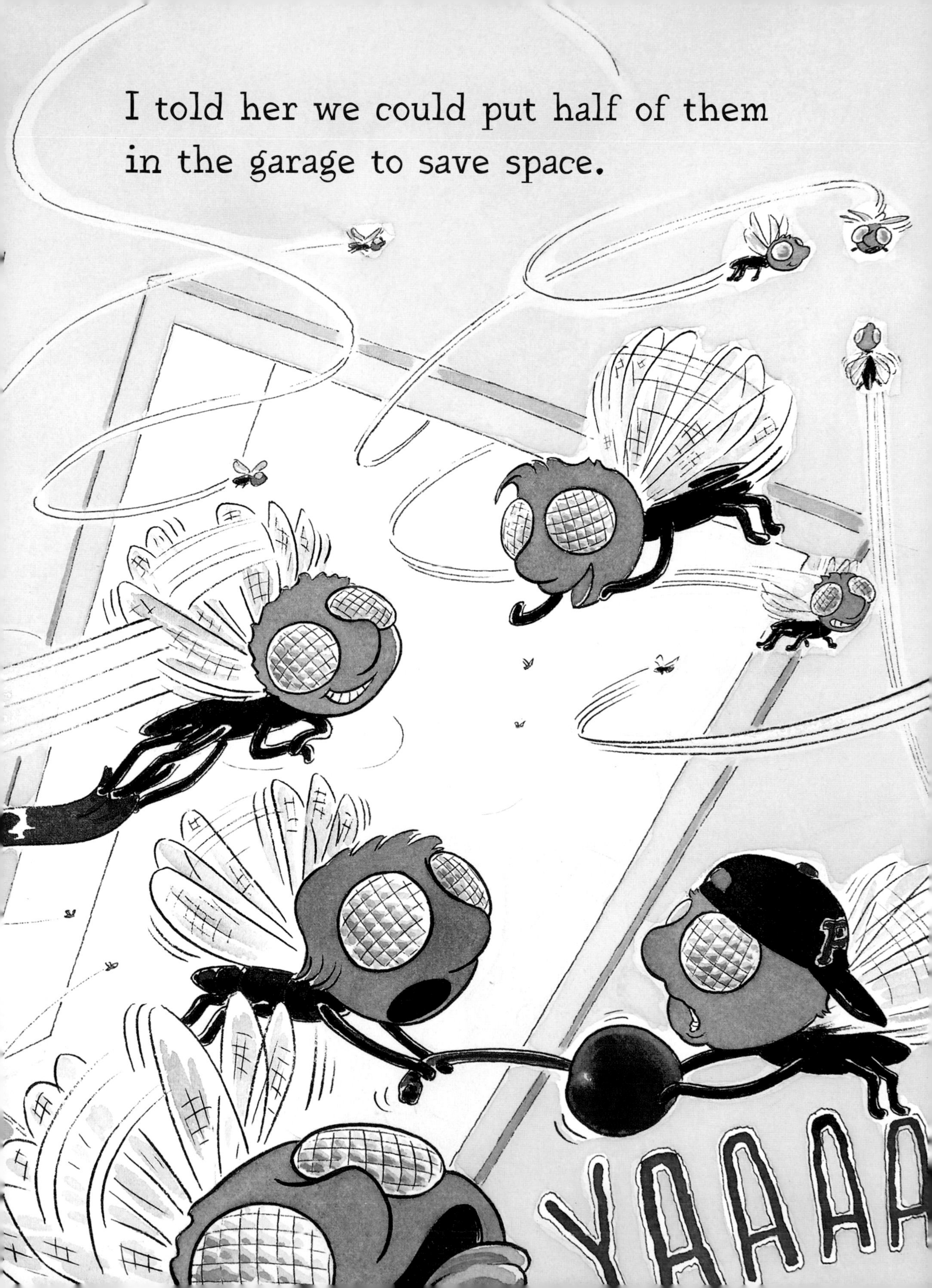

I'm having a time-out
in the garage right now.

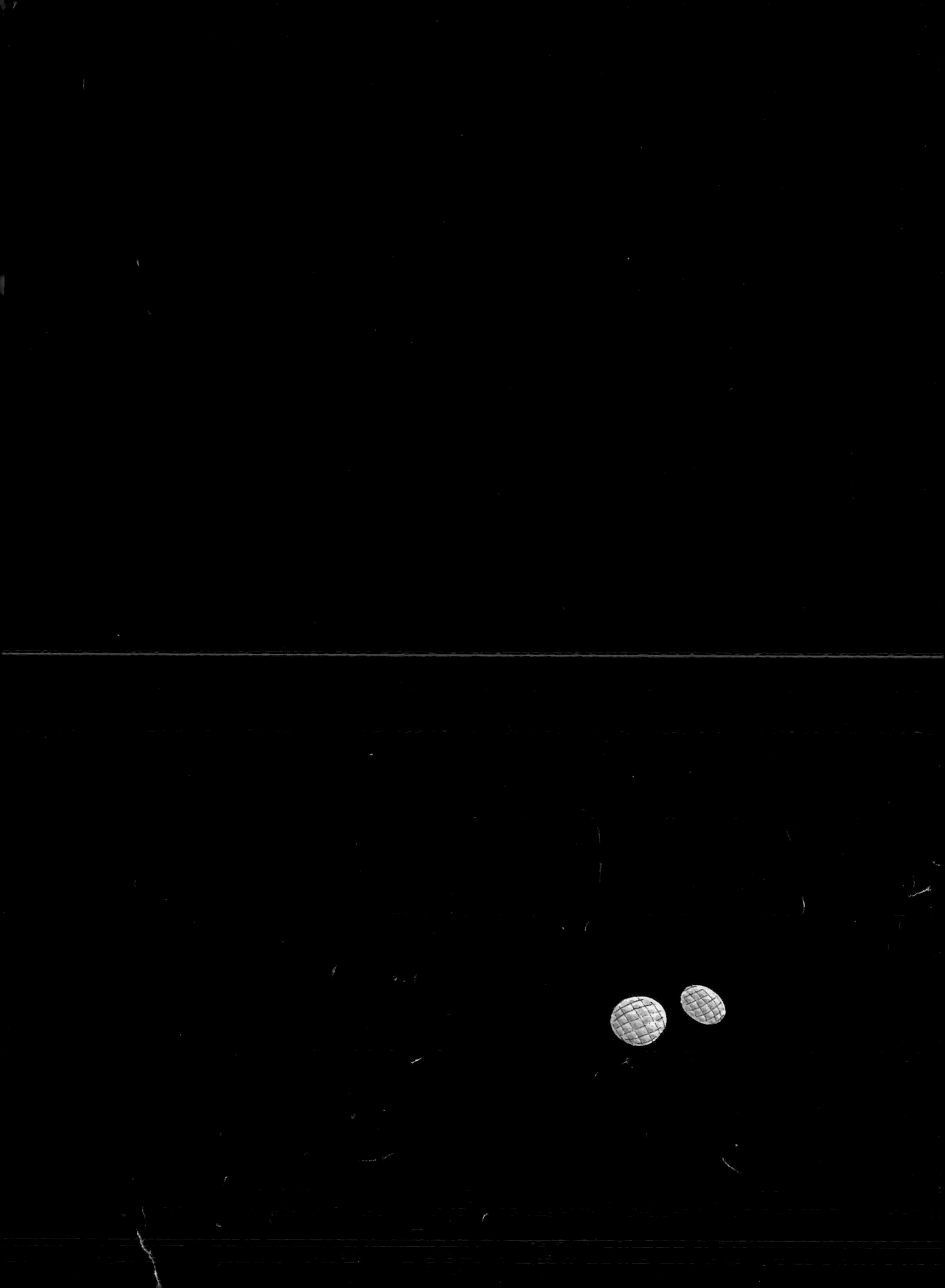

JULY 14
Spider's grandfather is so smart. He taught me flies were a very important part of the food chain. Very cool.
You're very important!

JULY 15

Worm sat me down and explained the food chain.

That is so not cool.

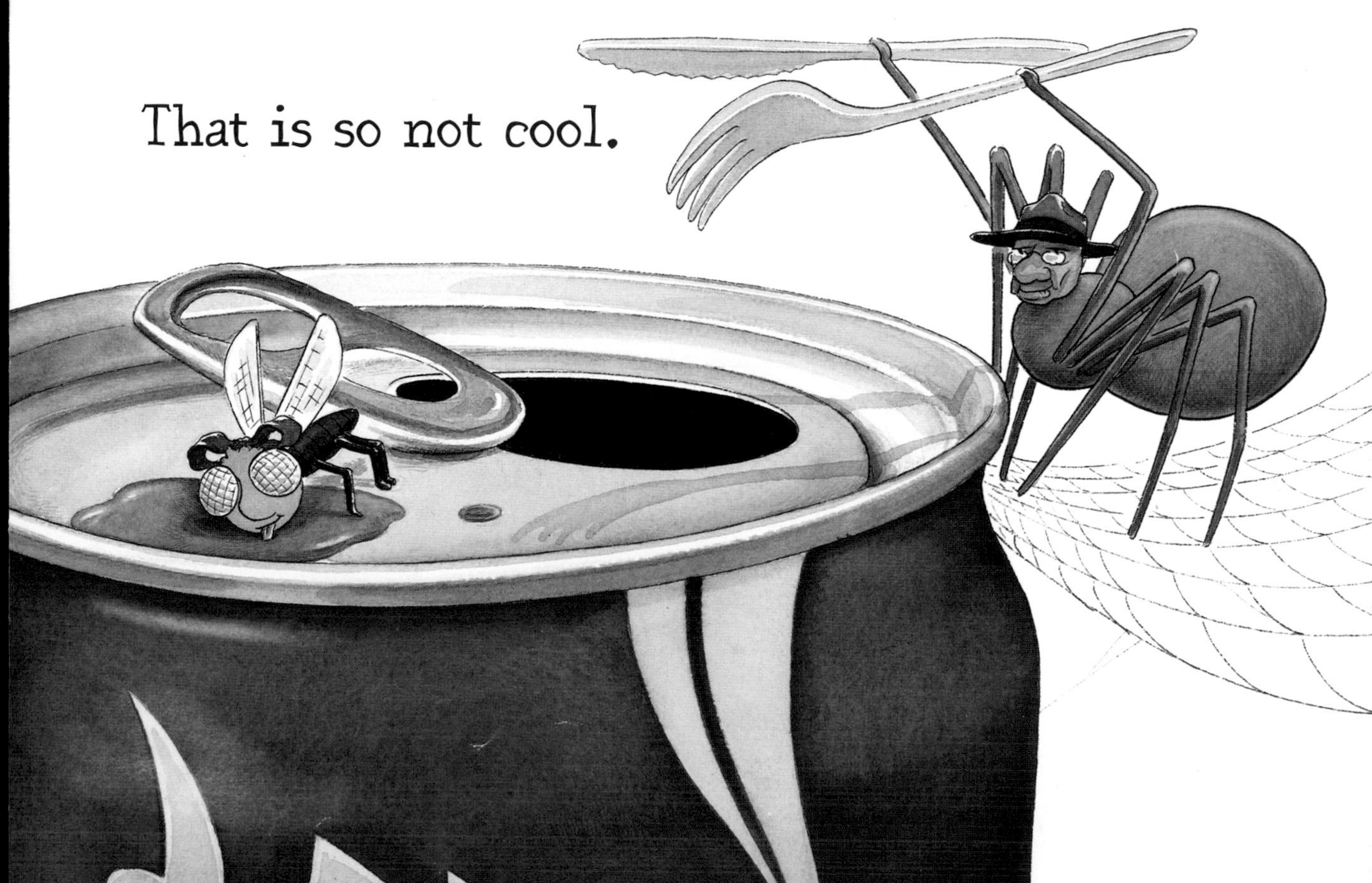

JULY 16

The babysitter came back last night.
She brought a frog.

When Mom and Dad got home,
we were all exactly where we were
when they left.

JULY 21

Why I would make a good superhero:

I have the most powerful flight muscles on the planet.

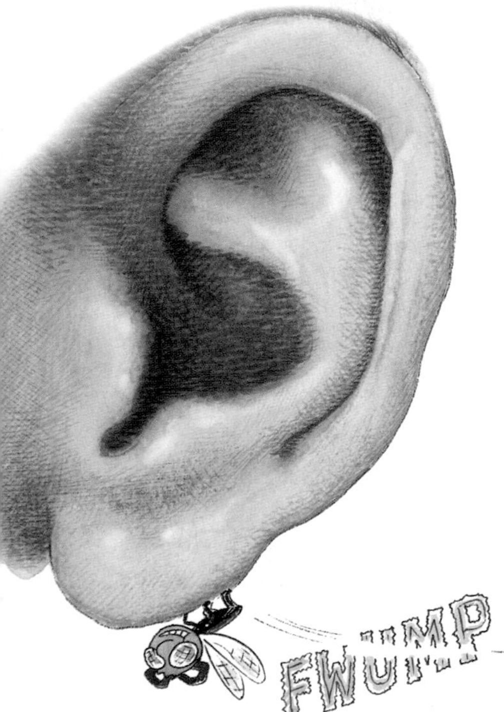

I can land upside down.

I can see in all directions at once.

Spider said, "Superheroes bend steel with their bare hands. You eat horse manure with your feet."

I never thought about it that way.

Today I learned that flies beat their wings 200 times per second.

No wonder I keep falling asleep in math.

JULY 23
I visited my aunt Rita today. She's been trapped on the wrong side of a screen for a week.
My word . . . how you've grown, dear.

AUGUST 1

I just know I would make an excellent superhero:

I have 4,000 lenses in each eye.

I can walk on walls.

I can change directions in flight faster than the blink of a human eye.

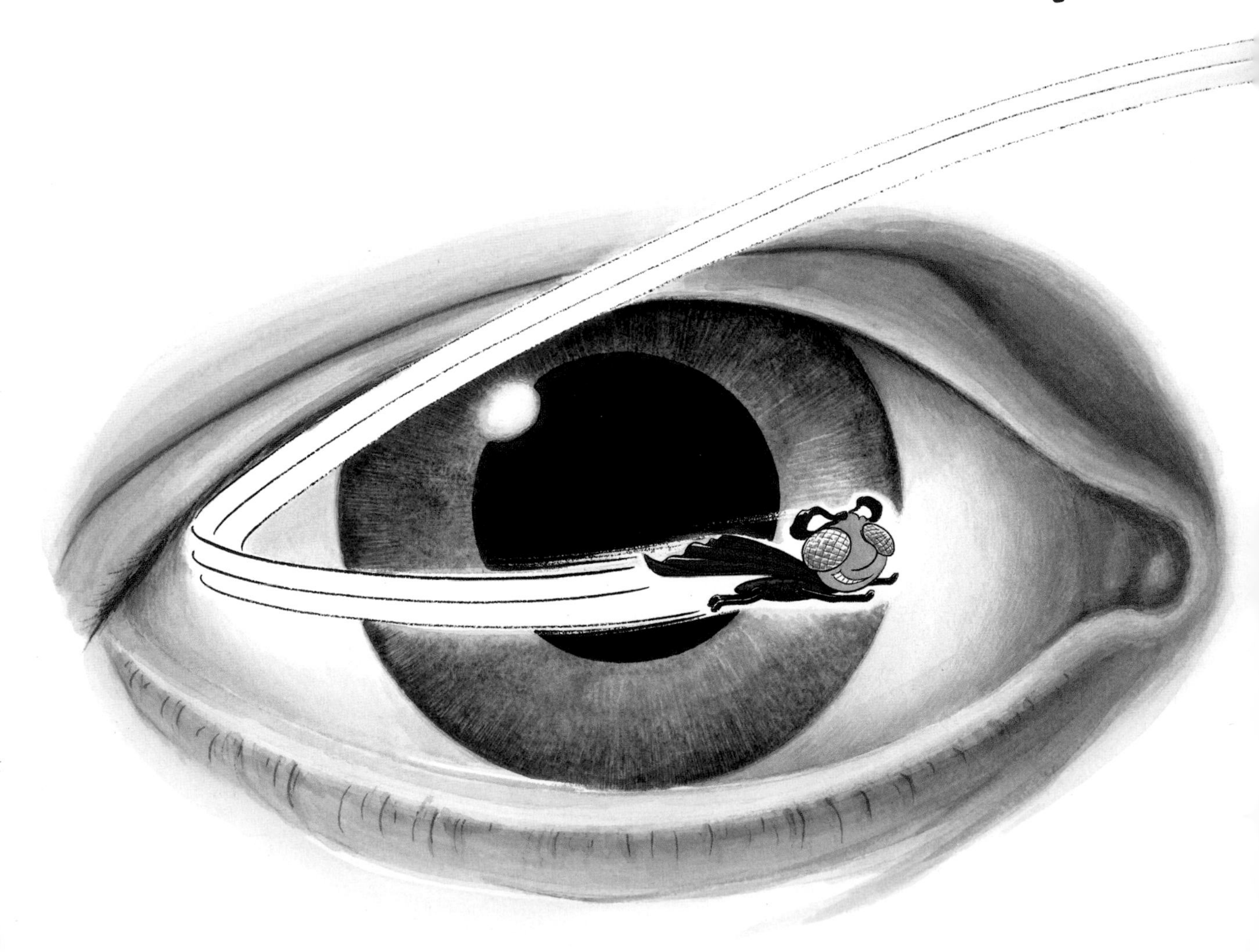

Spider said, "Superheroes save the world from outer-space villains. Your brain is the size of a sesame seed."

I never thought about it that way.

AUGUST 2

Today I told Worm and Spider that I could never be a superhero like I wanted.

Worm looked me right in the eyes and said, "The world needs all kinds of heroes."

Spider said, "I never thought about it that way."

Neither did I.

RONZO

Mom put this on the fridge.

Spider is soooooooo good at soccer!

Worm tunneled right through this marshmallow.

My favorite dinner!